T0145123

When Did God Make the Dinosaurs?

An Exploration of Science and Creation

Rhonda N. Smith

Illustrated by Kaileigh MacLeod

WestBow Press books may be ordered through booksellers or by contacting:

WestBow Press
A Division of Thomas Nelson & Zondervan
1663 Liberty Drive
Bloomington, IN 47403
www.westbowpress.com
1 (866) 928-1240

Interior Image Credit: Kaileigh MacLeod

ISBN: 978-1-9736-8813-6 (sc)
ISBN: 978-1-9736-8814-3 (e)

Library of Congress Control Number: 2020904784

Print information available on the last page.

WestBow Press rev. date: 04/20/2020

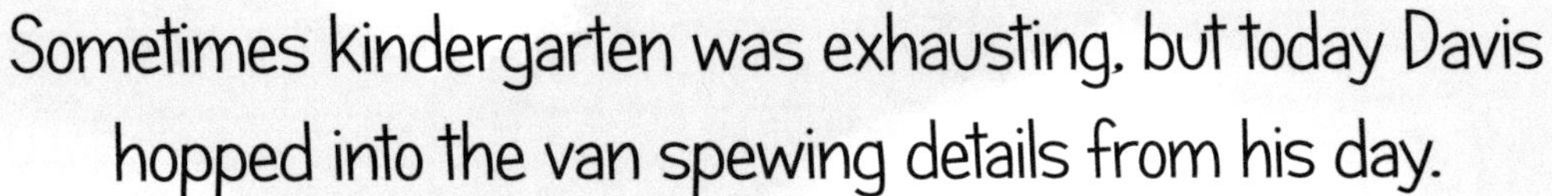
Sometimes kindergarten was exhausting, but today Davis hopped into the van spewing details from his day.

Hey Mom...Stevie said that the earth is billions of years old. I told him he was wrong 'cuz in Sunday school Miss Rosie said God made everything in 7 days!
Hello to you, too....sounds like an exciting day. You know, scientists study something called fossils to figure out how old things are...

I've seen fossils — in the dinosaur museum! When did God make the dinosaurs?
Good question. Let's look at what the Bible says when we get home, but first let me ask you a question.
Fossils
Fossils are the remains of a plant or animal preserved over a long time. Scientists study fossils to learn about the history of the earth.

When God told his people about the earth being made, what language do you think he was speaking?"
American?
You mean English?
God language!
Wait a minute — Cole, can you get your seatbelt on, please?

Actually, God spoke the language of the people in that land — the Hebrew language — so that they could understand him.
Does God speak Ameri... I mean English?
Sure, God speaks every language. And the Bible has been translated into English so that we can read it, too.
Hebrew has a different alphabet and is read from right to left.

The minivan had barely stopped when Davis leapt out and ran to the living room to pull the Children's Bible off the shelf. Mom and Cole met him on the couch...

...while Baby Molly played with Louie, their patient pup. Then, Mom had an idea.

Let's have an adventure! Imagine that our couch is a time machine. We'll go back and "see" what God told his people about making our world.

Yes! I'll grab binoculars to watch for dinosaurs!! And some snacks.
I'll get my blankie, and Louie — he loves trips.
Ok, are we ready to go? Time for the countdown....5, 4, 3, 2, 1...

BLAST OFF!

In the beginning, God created the heavens and the earth. (Genesis 1:1, NIRV)

The word ***"created"*** is translated from the Hebrew word ***"bara"*** and it means to make something new, something that did not exist before.

It sounds like the book we read about the Big Bang theory that explained that there was nothing and then, suddenly, matter (or stuff) appeared.

Is heaven where God lives?

Yes, but "the heavens" mentioned here is where the stars are — out in space.

This is what some scientists call the "Frame of Reference" or the state of things when this story began — God had already made the heavens and the earth — the universe.

The earth didn't have any shape. And it was empty. There was darkness over the surface of the waves. At that time, the Spirit of God was hovering over the waters. (Genesis 1:2, NIRV)

The Hebrew verb here translated as ***"hover"*** is the same word used to describe a mother bird brooding over her eggs, waiting for them to hatch.

Why do you think it was dark?
It was nighttime?
Maybe...but scientists tell us that planets often begin surrounded by a thick layer of gases and a blanket of dust and debris from outer space.

God said, "Let there be light." (Genesis 1:3a, NIRV)

Where is the light coming from?
But, God hasn't made that yet, has he?
The Sun!
Actually, what did we read in the first verse?

God made the heavens and earth — the sun was already made?
Yep! But, the light couldn't get through the thick blanket of gases.
הָיָה
"HAYA"
"**Let there be**" is translated from the Hebrew word "**haya**" which means "to come to pass." At this stage, the layer of gases began to thin, letting the light through. But, you may not have been able to see the sun yet from the surface of the earth – like on a really cloudy day.

There was evening and morning. It was day one. (Genesis 1:5b, NIRV)

12:00 a.m. → 12:00 p.m. → 12:00 a.m.

The word "day" can mean:

- Sunrise to sunset
- Sunset to sunset
- 24 hours
- A span of time

Actually, it's unusual to call the time from evening to morning a "day" – that sounds more like a night.

This may have been a poetic way to refer to the end of one time period and the beginning of another – like bookends.

God said, "Let there be a huge space between the waters. Let it separate water from water." ...God called the huge space "sky." (Genesis 1:6-8a, NIRV)

The water cycle is the story of how water moves in, on, and above the earth. Our atmosphere helps to keep the water in and not let it float out into space. All forms of water (ice, liquid, and gas) are essential to life on Earth.
It takes a very precise balance to have the sky hold in just the right amount of heat — not too cold, not too hot. This probably took a while to perfect — that was the second day, or time period.
I don't see any dinosaurs yet...

God said, 'Let the water under the sky be gathered into one place. Let dry ground appear." (Genesis 1:9a, NIRV)
Some scientists study the earth's surface and how it has changed over time. Lava erupting from volcanoes and something called plate tectonics helped form the land we know today."
Erupting volcanoes... Cool!

Scientists think that the land went from nothing to what it is now in about 4 billion years."
That's a long time!
God must be old... I bet he's old and a half!
Yes, getting the earth ready to be a good place for people to live took a very long time, but...
Plate Tectonic Theory says that the separate continents we see today were once a supercontinent called Pangaea.

Then God said, "Let the land produce plants." (Genesis 1:11a, NIRV)
....it was worth the wait.

How long did that take?
Well, I don't know exactly,
but some of the oldest trees date back to 370 million years ago.
No dinosaurs... but, look up there!

God said,"Let there be lights in the huge space of the sky. Let them separate the day from the night." (Genesis 1:14a, NIRV)
But, I thought God had already made the sun and stars?
Right, but now we can see them. The atmosphere (that thin blanket of gases) has gotten thin enough that we can see the stars.
There's the moon!
Some animals, like migrating birds, use the sun and stars to navigate where to go.

The Cambrian Explosion is based on the rather sudden appearance of more complex organisms in the fossil record.

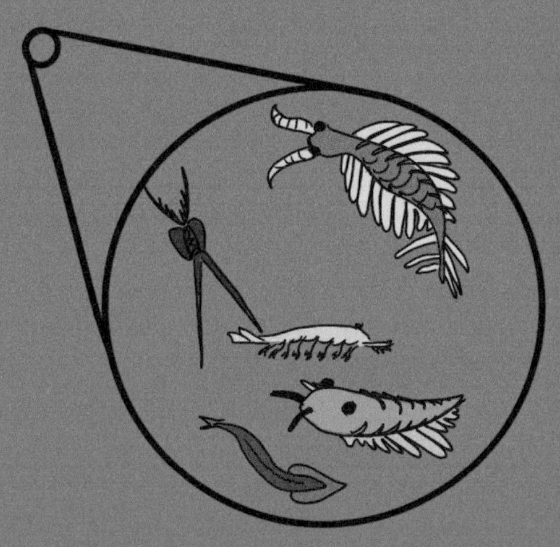

God said, "Let the seas be filled with living things. Let birds fly above the earth..." (Genesis 1:20a, NIRV)

Some dinosaurs flew...were they made on this "day"?
I'm glad you mentioned that, because the oldest dinosaur fossils date back to 100 million years before the earliest bird fossils found by paleontologists.
So, at least some of the dinosaurs lived during this time period.
Look... a dinosaur!

Whoa...watch out!

So, it looks like God made the dinosaurs on the same "day" as the birds and water animals...
I think there's evidence for that, at least for some of the dinosaurs.
Then, why didn't it say that in the Bible?
Paleontologists are scientists that study the fossil remains of prehistoric life.

What killed the dinosaurs? There are two main theories — a huge impact event, such as an asteroid hitting the earth, and very large volcanic eruptions. These two factors may have worked together to block out the sun, change the climate, and kill many species of that era, including the dinosaurs.

God said, "Let the land produce every kind of living creature." (Genesis 1:24a, NIRV)
Scientists breakdown the history of the earth into different time periods based on fossils. As they discover new evidence, it makes the story more clear.
It's not completely clear in the Bible when each different kind of animal came to be.
So far, the oldest mammal fossils that have been found are about 125 million years old.

How do you think we are made to be like God?
Then God said, "Let us make human beings so that they are like us." (Genesis 1:26a, NIRV)
We look like God?...But, what about Molly? She's a girl.
The Bible says that God created them male and female in his likeness – that means boys and girls. We might not look like God in our bodies, but we can love, think, and imagine and create things, like God does.

By the seventh day God had finished the work he had been doing.
So on that day he rested from all his work. (Genesis 2:2, NIRV)
I guess it's time to land this time machine!
Z Z Z
Awwwwwwww....

Yep, we're made in God's likeness. That means we are made to rest, too.
Can I take this book with me? I can't wait to tell Stevie about this at school tomorrow.
Look, Molly's sleepin' already!
Sure.
שבת
"Shabat" means to rest in Hebrew — "to cease")

About the Author:
Rhonda N. Smith

As a mother of 3, Rhonda had looked for books to read to her kids about how our world began that considered Biblical creation as well as scientific discovery. There were none to be found.

Not a scientist by training, she was inspired to create a picture book after taking a course on the earth's origins with the Reasons to Believe Institute. This was the first time that she had heard a theory that valued both science and the Biblical account. So, she worked with an artist friend to create this book for younger children to consider the Creation Theory Model – valuing both scientific discovery and Biblical understanding.

Rhonda now works as a non-profit director and shares an "emptying nest" with her husband in Pittsburgh. She is very grateful to her family and friends that provided feedback and editing to make this idea become a reality – especially Laurie C., Michael S., as well as M & C Smith.

Printed in the United States
By Bookmasters